The Case Of The
Disappearing Princess™

The New Adventures of MARY-KATE & ASHLEY™

The Case Of The
Disappearing Princess™

by Lisa Eisenberg

DUALSTAR PUBLICATIONS PARACHUTE PRESS

SCHOLASTIC INC.

New York   Toronto   London   Auckland   Sydney

DUALSTAR PUBLICATIONS PARACHUTE PRESS

Dualstar Publications
c/o Thorne and Company
1801 Century Park East
Los Angeles, CA 90067

Parachute Press
156 Fifth Avenue
Suite 325
New York, NY 10010

Published by Scholastic Inc.

With special thanks to Robert Thorne and Harold Weitzberg.

Printed in the U.S.A.
March 1999
ISBN: 0-439-06043-5
A B C D E F G H I J

WE'RE IN HOLLYWOOD!

"**T**here are movie stars *everywhere*!" I said to my twin sister, Ashley. "Look! Here comes Brittany Barlow!"

Brittany is the star of the hottest new movie, "The Disappearing Princess." Ashley and I won tickets to the premiere. That meant we would be among the very first kids to see the movie!

The crowd outside the theater was huge. There must have been two hundred kids there—and a bunch of grownups, too!

I was so excited that I didn't even mind waiting in a long line to get in. I knew that would surprise Ashley. She's the patient one. I like to jump right into things. But right then, I could have stood in line forever and stargazed!

Brittany walked down the long, red carpet toward the theater entrance. A mob of reporters and photographers followed her every step. Flashbulbs went off like crazy.

I read in a magazine that Brittany is ten years old—the same age as Ashley and me. But she was dressed like a grownup, in a light pink satin gown. And she had a long, pink scarf made of feathers draped around her shoulders. It's called a boa. Her dark hair was pinned up on top of her head. She looked so glamorous!

"Brittany!" A little girl in front of us was jumping up and down and waving at Brittany. "It's *me*, Jessica. Don't you remember me? I sent you ten fan letters!"

Brittany glanced at the little girl as she

passed by. Then she stuck her nose in the air and walked into the theater.

Ashley frowned. "Boy, Brittany isn't very friendly."

"You're right," I agreed. "But I don't even care if she's snobby. I'm too excited about being here."

"I still can't believe we won tickets to the premiere!" I added. "It's a good thing I noticed that contest entry form on the back of the cereal box—"

"Hey!" Ashley laughed. "Who wrote our winning essay: Why I Love the Mystery of Princess Anna?"

"You did," I said. "Thanks, Ashley!"

Ashley and I both love the story of Princess Anna. "The Disappearing Princess" movie is about her life. She was a real Russian princess who lived many years ago. One summer, Princess Anna disappeared while her family was at one of their vacation castles. Her family searched for her for years. But the only thing they ever found was her favorite doll. The mystery of her disappearance was never solved.

"Mary-Kate! Ashley!" A loud voice screamed at us from somewhere in the crowd.

I knew that voice! "It's Patty O'Leary," I said to Ashley. "What is *she* doing here?"

Ashley shrugged. "She must have written a winning essay, too."

Patty is in our class at school. She also lives next door to us. She's the most spoiled person I've ever met. Ashley and I nicknamed her "Princess Patty" because she acts like she's better than everybody else.

I stood on tiptoe and looked around. Sure enough, there was Patty, waving at us. She wore a red dress with glittery sequins all over it. Her brown hair was wrapped in a fancy bun. She was standing at the front of the line.

"Too bad you're way in the *back* of the line!" Patty shouted at us. "Hope you brought binoculars to watch the movie!"

It figured that Princess Patty was one of the first kids on line!

Finally the line started to move forward. Yes! It was time for the premiere!

"I can't wait to see Princess Anna's doll," Ashley said. "I heard it's going to be on display in the lobby."

"Wow!" I gasped. Princess Anna's doll—the one she left behind when she disappeared. We were actually going to see it!

"I wish we could go faster," Jessica whined to the teenage boy standing next to her. Her curly red hair bobbed up and down as she bounced impatiently. "I want to see the doll *now*, Donald! Can't we go any *faster?*"

"Stop whining, Jessica!" Donald shouted at her. "It's bad enough I have to take my kid sister to this dumb movie!"

"*Next!*" a grumpy voice said in my ear. I turned and saw the ticket taker staring at me. She had a blond ponytail and green nail polish. Her palm was stretched out toward us.

Ashley and I handed her the bright-orange tickets we'd received in the mail.

The ticket taker stared at us. "Aren't you two those twin detectives? Your names are Mary-Alice and Annie, right?"

"Mary-Kate and Ashley," Ashley told her.

The ticket taker had our names wrong. But she was right about one thing—we *are* detectives. Ashley and I run the Olsen and Olsen Mystery Agency out of the attic of our house in California. We love mysteries—and that's another reason why we love the story of Princess Anna so much!

The line moved forward again. We walked into the theater. It was beautiful. The ceilings were high, with gold angels painted on them. The floor was made out of shiny white marble.

All the kids formed a new line to see Princess Anna's doll. Everyone was standing on tiptoe.

"*Donald!*" the little girl, Jessica, whined again. "Everyone's taller than me! I can't get a peek at the doll!"

Donald ignored her.

"No one even believes that I'm really here," Jessica said. "All my friends think I'm lying about going to the premiere and getting to see the doll!"

Donald rolled his eyes. "That's it! I can't take another minute of your complaining. I'm going to get some popcorn." He stepped out of line. When he turned sideways, he almost hit me in the face with his huge backpack! And his big boots left a trail of black scuff marks on the shiny white floor.

"What a mess!" Ashley whispered to me.

"Donald!" Jessica cried. "Come back! I just thought of how I can prove I was really here!"

I really wanted to hear how she planned to prove it. But Donald just rolled his eyes at her again and kept walking. So Jessica didn't say anything else.

Ashley and I reached the glass display case that held Princess Anna's doll. "Ohhhh," I breathed. "She's beautiful."

The doll wasn't very big—about a foot tall. She was made out of delicate porcelain. Her eyes were deep blue. Her black hair was long and curly.

Above her left eyebrow was a little crack. I probably wouldn't even have noticed it if I hadn't read about it in a magazine. It happened when one of Anna's older brothers threw a ball and accidentally knocked the doll off a table onto the floor.

A beautiful gold and diamond crown sat on the doll's head. Her dress was made out of shiny pink satin and antique white lace. I loved the tiny, jeweled slippers she wore on her dainty little feet.

I wished I could touch the beautiful doll. But she was safely locked inside the glass display case.

"Good afternoon," a short, bald man said to the crowd. "I am Mr. Gudov. I am the owner of Princess Anna's doll."

He pointed to a tall, blond woman next to him. "This is Ruska, my assistant. The doll will be on display throughout the showing of the movie and for one hour afterwards."

A man in a guard's uniform stood by the display case. He had a name tag on. It said: BORIS — SECURITY GUARD.

Ruska announced that it was time for the premiere. Everyone began walking into the theater. We followed the line inside.

"Ashley, look!" I said, pointing to the middle rows of seats. "There's the roped-off section where all the movie stars sit!" I could see a lot of my favorite celebrities!

"Wow!" Ashley said. "But we'd better stop looking at them and start finding seats — before all the good ones are gone."

We climbed over a bunch of people's legs and sank into two seats.

"This is *totally* unfair!" someone said loudly in my ear.

I turned to my left — and there was

Princess Patty!

"What's totally unfair, Patty?" I asked.

"I got this good seat because I was first in line! It's not fair that *you two* got good seats, too!" she complained. "You were way in back."

Ashley and I grinned at each other. Then Ashley glanced at her watch. "The movie doesn't start for another five minutes. If we hurry, we can still get popcorn. Patty, will you save our seats?"

"Oh, all right," Patty grumbled.

"Do you want popcorn, too, Patty?" I asked her—just to be polite.

She shook her head. "And risk getting popcorn grease on this one-of-a-kind designer gown? No way."

I rolled my eyes. Ashley and I hurried up the aisle and pushed open the double doors. The lobby was deserted, since everyone was seated inside the theater.

"Hey," I said. "Let's take one more look at the doll and then get our popcorn! The display is just around the corner."

Ashley's eyes lit up. We dashed toward the display case.

I stopped short. My mouth dropped open.

Ashley gasped.

"Oh, no!" I cried. "The Princess Anna doll is gone!"

THAT'S THE TICKET!

I couldn't believe it. The doll's display case was empty!

"*What?*" I heard a woman shriek. I turned and saw Ruska, the doll's owner's assistant. She raced over to Ashley and me.

She stared at the empty display case. "Oh no!" she cried. "The doll has been stolen! How could this happen?"

Ruska looked around the deserted lobby. "Where is Boris, the guard?" she yelled. "He was supposed to watch the doll at all times!"

Boris rushed over. "I left the doll for only five minutes!" he said. "I had to use the bathroom." Then he noticed the empty case. His face turned very pale. "The doll! It is gone! I'm so sorry!"

"Boy, is he in trouble!" I whispered to Ashley.

"Never mind your excuses!" Ruska screamed at him. "These children stole Princess Anna's doll!"

What?

I stared at Ashley. I couldn't believe it. Ruska thought *we* took the doll?

"No!" I exclaimed. "We didn't steal the doll! I promise!"

"That's right!" Ashley declared. "My sister is telling the truth."

"Wait a minute," Ruska said. She stepped closer to us. "I recognize you two from a magazine I read. You're those twin detectives, aren't you?"

Ashley nodded. "I'm Ashley Olsen, and this

is my sister, Mary-Kate."

"Please say you will help me!" Ruska cried. "I need you to find Princess Anna's doll—fast! Before my boss discovers she's missing." She covered her eyes with her hands. "Or he'll fire me—and the guard, too!" she shrieked.

Ashley looked at me. "It wasn't very nice of Ruska to accuse us of stealing the doll," she whispered.

"I know," I agreed. "But maybe she was just really upset."

"Maybe," Ashley said. "But there's something else. If we start investigating now, we'll miss the movie!"

I bit my lip. I really didn't want to miss the movie premiere. But Ruska needed our help!

"We can see the movie when it comes out in regular theaters," I told Ashley. "I think we should help Ruska. I say we take the case."

Ashley nodded. She turned to Ruska. "How do you think someone got the doll out of the display case?" she asked.

That was a good question. I studied the case. The glass wasn't broken. And the case was still locked.

Ruska took her hands away from her face and stared at us. "I don't know!" she said, frowning. "But someone did! Please—you have to find that doll. It was owned by Princess Anna herself."

Ruska leaned very close to us. "It's a one of a kind—and very valuable," she whispered. "People all over the world would love to own it. It's worth a million dollars!"

Ashley and I exchanged glances. A million dollars was a lot of money. This was serious!

"First of all, who has keys to the display case?" I asked Ruska.

"Besides Mr. Gudov, the doll's owner," Ruska told us, "I am the only other person who has a key."

"Did you maybe lend your key to anyone?" Ashley asked.

"Of course not!" Ruska snapped. She

looked shocked.

"Thanks for the information, Ruska," I said. "Ashley and I need to investigate around the display case. Try not to worry."

"I'll try," Ruska said. She held out her hands to us. "Thank you so much for helping me. I'll be in the back room doing some paperwork— if I can even concentrate!" She and Boris walked away in different directions.

I circled the display case. There had to be clues around there somewhere.

I looked behind the case. Nothing there.

I looked on one side of the display case. Nothing there.

I peeked on the other side.

Hey! What was that?

I bent down to take a closer look at some bits of orange cardboard. They lay in a heap on the floor.

"Ashley," I whispered. "I found something!"

Ashley hurried over. She kneeled down. "These are ticket stubs—to the movie premiere!" she said.

"This is our first clue," I said.

"Who could have dropped these here?" Ashley asked.

"I know!" I exclaimed. "Only one person would have a whole stack of ticket stubs. That grumpy ticket taker with the green nails!"

"You're right," Ashley said.

"She probably dropped these tickets here by accident," I said. "While she was stealing the doll!"

"She's definitely our first suspect," Ashley said. "We'd better go talk to her."

I picked up the ticket stubs and put them inside my little purse. I wished I had the things I usually carried around with me—like plastic evidence bags and my mini tape-recorder.

But Ashley and I were all dressed up for a movie premiere, so we had not been able to bring our usual things with us. I really wanted to check the display case for fingerprints. But without our detective kit, we couldn't!

Luckily, Ashley had her detective's notebook with her—for getting autographs! She pulled it out and wrote SUSPECTS on a blank page. Underneath that, she wrote: TICKET TAKER.

"Let's look around here some more before we talk to the ticket taker," I said. "Maybe we'll find more clues."

"Good idea," Ashley said.

I hiked up my dress so I could get down on my hands and knees. I searched all around.

And then I saw something very strange.

"Ashley!" I cried. "You're not going to believe what *else* I just found!"

3

THE MYSTERY FEATHER

"**I**t's a pink feather," I said.

I picked the fluffy pink feather up and turned it over in my palm. Ashley leaned over and stared at it.

"I know I saw feathers like that somewhere tonight," she said. "But where?"

"I did, too," I said. "But I can't remember either."

We both thought hard for a minute.

"We could really use Clue right now!" I said. "Her nose could track down where these clues came from right away!"

Clue is our basset hound. She's no ordinary dog. She's such a good sniffer, we made her part of our detective team. But Clue didn't get invited to the movie premiere!

Ashley opened her purse and dropped the feather inside. "Okay," she said. "First, let's talk to that ticket taker. Then, let's try to remember where we saw pink feathers like that tonight."

"Good idea," I said. We went back outside the theater.

The blond ticket taker was still sitting in her ticket booth. She was reading a comic book and chewing bubble gum.

"Excuse me," Ashley said to her. "Can we ask you a few questions?"

The girl didn't even look up. She blew a giant bubble. Then she turned another page in her comic.

I cleared my throat loudly. "Excuse me, could we please ask you a few questions?"

The ticket taker sighed. She blew another huge bubble and popped it with a long, green fingernail. "Yeah?" she said.

I noticed she was wearing a little name tag. It said: HI! MY NAME IS KRISTEN. HOW CAN I HELP YOU?

I opened my purse and took out the stack of tickets. "We found these in the lobby," I told Kristen. "By the doll's display case."

"So?" Kristen asked, flipping another page in the comic book.

"Do you happen to know how they got there?" Ashley asked. "It's really important."

"I don't have a clue," Kristen said. "And I couldn't care less, either."

She put down her comic. "How come you two want to know anyway? Why are you asking me all these dumb questions?"

"We're detectives, remember?" Ashley told her. "We're working on an investigation."

Kristen shrugged and blew another bubble. "Don't look at me," she said. "I didn't drop those ticket stubs. I've been stuck in this booth all night. I have to sit here during the whole movie in case somebody comes in late!"

Kristen stuck out her lip. "I really wanted to see the movie, too. But I'm not allowed!"

"Can you think of anyone else who would have ticket stubs?" Ashley asked.

"No," Kristen replied, blowing another huge bubble.

Ashley pulled out her detective notebook from her purse. She made some notes.

I thought of another question.

"Kristen, did you see anyone run out of the theater? He or she might have been carrying a bag or a backpack."

"No, I didn't see anybody," Kristen said.

"Are you sure?" Ashley asked. "You've been reading your comic book. Maybe someone left and you didn't notice."

Kristin shook her head. "Are you kidding?" she asked. "That dumb door to the theater makes a really loud popping noise every time it opens or closes. I would have heard it if someone left."

"Is there another way out of the theater besides this door?" I asked.

"I have no idea," Kristen replied.

We thanked Kristen and walked to a bench right in front of the theater entrance.

"Do you think she's telling the truth?" I asked Ashley. "She said she didn't leave the booth all night."

"I don't know," Ashley said. "She's mad that she didn't get to see the movie. That could be her motive for stealing the doll, I guess. What do you think?"

"I think we'd better watch her," I said. "We can't rule her out yet."

Ashley tapped her pencil on the notebook. "She also said she didn't see or hear anyone leave the theater."

"That means whoever stole the doll is still inside," I replied.

"Then the doll is definitely still in the theater, too!" Ashley responded.

"Right!" I agreed. "Wait a minute," I added. "Kristen told us she didn't know if there's another exit. Maybe the thief slipped out a back door."

"True," Ashley agreed. "Let's check out the theater. Then we'll investigate the pink feather we found. Maybe it will lead us to another suspect. If only we could figure out where it came from!" She frowned and tapped her fingers on her notebook.

I thought hard. But nothing came to me.

And then something caught my eye.

It was the movie poster of "The Disappearing Princess" on the theater wall. It showed Brittany Barlow sitting on a throne.

I jumped up and gasped. "I just figured out where that pink feather came from!" I shouted.

4

STAR SEARCH!

"Where?" Ashley asked, jumping up from the bench.

"Look at this poster of Brittany Barlow," I told her. "You'll see."

Ashley took one look at the poster and let out a shriek. "The *boa!* The pink boa she's wearing around her shoulders! It's made out of pink feathers."

Ashley pulled the feather out of her purse and held it up next to the poster. "It looks like the same kind," she said.

"Brittany was wearing that same boa when she arrived at the theater tonight!" I exclaimed. "The feather we found by the display case had to come from her boa!"

"I think you're right," Ashley agreed. "We checked out the whole crowd while waiting on line. And no one else had anything made of pink feathers." Ashley frowned. "But why would Brittany steal the doll?" she murmured. "What could her motive be?"

"I don't know," I admitted. "But even if we don't know her motive, she's still a suspect. The feather is a big clue!"

"You're right. We should question her right away," Ashley said. "But she's watching the premiere—of her own movie!"

I looked at my watch. "The movie started about twenty minutes ago," I said. "That means Brittany won't come out for another hour and ten minutes."

"We could wait for the movie to end," Ashley said. "Then we could stand by the exit for the VIP section. Brittany will walk right by us. We can talk to her then."

Ashley took out her detective notebook. She added Brittany Barlow's name to our list of suspects.

"Let's head back inside," I said. "We can look for back exits."

The minute we pulled the door open, Ruska rushed up to us.

"Ashley! Mary-Kate!" she cried. "I've been looking for you! Have you found my precious doll yet?"

"Not yet," I said. "But we have suspects. We'll find out more in about an hour."

"Oh, no!" Ruska looked upset. "My boss, Mr. Gudov, will be back after the movie ends. You have to find the doll before he discovers what has happened. Or Boris and I will get fired!"

Ruska sounded as if she were ready to cry. "It's okay," I told her. I patted her hand. "We'll try to speed things up."

Ruska gave Ashley and me a small smile.

Then she rushed away.

"We have to find Brittany right away. We can't wait for the movie to end," I told Ashley.

"But will she talk to us?" Ashley asked. "She's a famous movie star. And she didn't seem very nice, either."

"I don't know," I said. "We have to try, though!"

Ashley nodded. We headed for the double doors. We quietly pushed them open and peered inside.

"Hey!" someone called to us. "Shut that door! You're letting in the light!"

"Sorry," I whispered. We slipped inside and closed the door as fast as we could.

I turned around and stared up at the movie. Brittany, as Princess Anna, was on the screen.

She was wearing a filmy white dress. She was running through a misty field at night. She looked beautiful and mysterious.

"Why is she running?" I asked Ashley. "Is somebody chasing her?"

Ashley yanked on my arm. "Mary-Kate!" she whispered. "Stop watching the movie! We have to find Brittany Barlow!"

Ashley and I tiptoed down the aisle to the roped-off VIP section. Even in the dark, I could see the shiny dresses of the actresses in the VIP seats. Everyone was staring up at the movie screen. I wanted to do the same thing!

"Where is Brittany's seat?" Ashley whispered to me.

"I think she was in the front row of the VIP section," I whispered back. "Ashley, look! There's Gregory Dumont! He's the hottest move star in Hollywood! And Linda Lawrence is right next to him. She plays the Queen in 'The Disappearing Princess'!"

"Shhh!" Ashley ordered in a low voice. "Stop stargazing. Look for Brittany Barlow."

We tiptoed further down the aisle. We came to the front row of the roped-off section. Everyone was so into the movie that no one even noticed us.

"Brittany's seat should be on the aisle in this row," I whispered.

"Are you sure?" Ashley whispered back. "I don't see her at all."

Then Ashley bent down and peered at something in the darkness. "Mary-Kate! Look at this!"

I leaned over. Ashley was staring at a gold name tag on the back of one of the plush seats. The gold was so bright that it glowed in the dark. The name tag said: BRITTANY BARLOW.

"The seat is empty," Ashley whispered in my ear. "Brittany Barlow is missing from her own premiere!"

BRITTANY *BARLOW*

Ashley and I stumbled back up the dark aisle. When we came out of the theater, we blinked in the bright lobby light.

"Well, now we know," I said.

"Now we know what?" Ashley asked.

"Who stole the doll!" I replied. "It was Brittany Barlow! Maybe she thinks she deserves to have the doll because she was Princess Anna in the movie."

Ashley put a finger to her lips. "Mary-Kate," she said. "Keep your voice down. You could get in trouble talking about Brittany like that. She's a big movie star."

"And she's probably a thief!" I said. "Why else wouldn't she be watching the premiere of her own movie? She sneaked out of the theater and stole Princess Anna's doll!"

"You could be right," Ashley said. "But we don't know for sure. We need proof."

"So we have to find her right away," I said. "She has to be here in the theater somewhere. Remember what Kristen said? No one left the theater since the movie started."

"You're right," Ashley said. "I heard that Brittany has her own dressing room right here in the theater. Let's find it. Maybe she's in there."

"And remember," I said, "Even if she doesn't have the doll, that doesn't mean she's *not* the thief. She could have hidden it somewhere in the theater."

"Good point," Ashley said. "Come on—we have a movie star to track down!"

There was a long hallway off the lobby. As we walked down it, we passed Boris, the doll's guard. He was carrying a red velvet cloth toward the display case.

"Ruska wants me to cover it," he said gloomily. "So no one will notice that the doll is gone." He heaved a huge sigh and walked away.

"He probably thinks he's going to get fired," I whispered. "He seems so nice, too."

"I know," Ashley replied. "That's why we have to find the doll soon—so Boris and Ruska won't get fired."

We continued down the hallway. I checked out all the signs on the doors. FILMS. PROJECTORS. MOVIE POSTERS. PRIVATE OFFICE. But I didn't see any doors with a sign for movie stars.

We turned a corner. WHAM! We almost crashed into a glamorous woman. She wore a black silk blouse and slim back pants. Her high-heeled boots were made of shiny black leather.

"Excuse me," Ashley said to the woman. "Do you know where Brittany Barlow's dressing room is?"

"I'd better know," the woman said, smiling. "I'm her agent and manager, Ginger. You girls must be some of her little fans. But I'm afraid you're out of luck if you were hoping to meet her. Brittany is not in a very good mood right now. Sorry."

I looked at Ashley. Maybe Brittany was in a bad mood because she felt guilty for stealing the doll!

"We're big fans," Ashley said. "We saw that she wasn't in her seat. So we came out to try and find her. Do you think we could just go in and quickly ask her for her autograph?"

Ginger frowned. "I guess so," she said. "She's having a neck rub right now. Her dressing room is two doors down on the left. But remember—she's in a bad mood. She might not feel like signing autographs."

"Why isn't she watching the movie?" I

asked. "Doesn't she want to see her own movie premiere?"

"She already saw it," Ginger explained. "The studio let her see an early screening. She was going to watch it again tonight, but she got a horrible headache as soon as she entered the theater."

Ginger pulled out a small mirror and lipstick. "Brittany's head was pounding so badly that she didn't even stop to look at the doll. She just came straight here. She's been getting a neck rub ever since!"

Ginger carefully applied red lipstick. Then she blotted her lips. "Please excuse me, girls," she said. "I have to go meet with some reporters. They want to interview me about Brittany's career."

We thanked Ginger and watched her walk away. "Wow," I said. "If she's telling the truth, Brittany didn't steal the doll."

"That's right," Ashley said. "Because she went straight into her dressing room and has been there ever since."

"Maybe Ginger is lying, though," I said. "Maybe she knows Brittany stole the doll. She could be lying to protect her!"

"We'd better question Brittany," Ashley responded.

We walked to the door Ginger pointed out. The door had a gold star on it. BRITTANY BARLOW was written on the star in fancy script.

Ashley started to knock on the door. But then it opened. A woman in a white nurse's uniform came out into the hallway.

"Excuse me," I said to her. "Did you just give Brittany Barlow a neck rub?"

"Brittany *Brat*low is more like it!" the woman answered. She held up her hands. "I've been in there rubbing that pint-sized movie star's neck for well over half an hour! My fingers have cramps!"

"Ingrid!" Brittany's voice called out through the open door. "Come rub my feet for a while! Now I have a foot ache. Ingrid? Ingrid!"

Ingrid put a finger to her lips. "You never saw me," she whispered to us. Then she ran away down the hall.

Ashley and I smiled and walked away from Brittany's door. "Well, I guess that means Ginger was telling the truth," Ashley said. "Ingrid has been rubbing Brittany's neck since before the movie started."

I nodded. "We have to cross Brittany off our list," I said.

Ashley opened the detective notebook. She drew a line through Brittany's name.

"Wait a minute," Ashley said, frowning. "There's something I don't get. Ginger said Brittany didn't even stop to look at the doll."

"Right," I prompted.

"So how did that pink feather end up by the doll's display case?" Ashley asked.

Hmmm. "Good question," I said. "And if Kristen never left the ticket booth all night, how did those ticket stubs end up there, too?"

"We have a lot more investigating to do,"

Ashley said. "This case just doesn't make any sense."

Then I thought of something. I snapped my fingers. "Wait a minute!" I said. "I know who did it! I know who took Princess Anna's doll!"

THE DOLL NAPPER!

Ashley grabbed my arm. "Who, Mary-Kate?" she cried. "Who took the doll?"

"Jessica did it!" I said excitedly. "That little red-haired girl who was in front of us on line."

"You mean the one who was whining?" Ashley asked. "The girl with her teenage brother?"

"Yeah!" I said. "Remember what we heard her say? That her friends would never believe she was at this premiere!"

"Right," Ashley said. "So?"

"And then," I went on, "she said something else. She said she'd thought of a way to prove to them that she was really here!"

"That's right," Ashley said. "But Donald walked away right then. So she didn't finish what she was going to say."

"Well, I'll bet she was going to say that she should steal the doll!" I exclaimed. "That would be all the proof she would need to show her friends she was really here."

"But it's not all the proof *we* need," Ashley reminded me. She ran her fingers through her hair. "Jessica definitely has a motive. She *could* be the thief. But we need proof."

Ashley opened the detective notebook and added Jessica's name to our suspect list.

"We have to question Jessica," I said. "Let's go into the theater and find her."

"We'll never find her in the dark, Mary-Kate," Ashley pointed out. "She's not in the VIP section like Brittany Barlow."

"You're right," I said. I frowned. "I guess we

have to wait until the movie ends. Ruska will have to understand."

"We have just under an hour. We can use the time to check out the rest of the theater," Ashley said. "Because if Jessica *did* steal the doll, she might have hidden it somewhere."

"Yeah," I agreed. "And she's probably planning to take it when she leaves."

"Okay," Ashley said. "We'll check out the theater, then we'll wait by the doors for Jessica and Donald to come out."

"Let's start searching!" I said.

Ashley and I walked around the whole building. First we looked for back exits. We found one—but it was locked.

Then we looked into every corner for the doll. We got down on our hands and knees. We looked under every bench and chair. We even felt in the dirt inside the potted plants.

But by the end of the hour, we had found: nothing!

Ashley glanced at a clock on the wall of the

lobby. "We need to go stand by the exit now," she said. "Donald and Jessica will be out in a minute or two."

We hurried over to the double doors. They swung open and a big crowd of people spilled out into the lobby. Everyone was smiling and talking about how great the movie was. Too bad Ashley and I never even saw it!

We spotted Jessica and Donald in the crowd. Patty was right behind them.

"Jessica!" I called. "Jessica and Donald! Could you come over here for a minute?"

Jessica looked confused. "Do I know you?" she asked. "How come you know my name?"

Donald peered at me. Then he stared at Ashley. "Wow," he said. "Am I seeing double, or are you two twins? Are you double trouble, or what?"

Ashley and I smiled. We've heard lots of twin jokes before!

"We want to ask you something," I said.

"Jessica," Ashley began, "while we were

waiting on line, we heard you say something interesting. You said that you knew a way to prove to your friends you were really here."

Now Jessica looked *really* confused. "What?" she said.

"Could you tell us what your plan was?" I asked.

"I guess so," Jessica replied. "I remembered that Donald brought a camera. He wanted to take pictures of the movie stars. So I figured he could take a picture of me standing next to the doll's display case! Then I could show the picture to everyone at school."

"Did Donald take the picture?" I asked.

"No!" Jessica complained. "I asked him to when we took our seats. I asked about a hundred times before the movie started. But then he got really mad at me and stormed off!" Jessica turned to her brother. "Donald! Let's take a picture of the doll *now!*"

"I'm afraid you can't do that," Ashley said. "The doll has been stolen."

"S-stolen?" Jessica stammered. Her lower lip trembled. Tears welled up in her eyes.

"Stolen?" someone in the lobby echoed. They must have overheard us. "Princess Anna's doll was stolen?"

Oh, no! Now the secret was out!

Ashley nudged me in the ribs. "We have to solve this mystery fast!" she whispered.

"Jessica," I began. "I'm not accusing you of anything, but I have to ask. Did you take the doll? That would be a good way to prove to your friends you were really here."

Jessica's eyes opened wide. "What? No way!" she shrieked. "I didn't! You can see for yourself I don't have it. I don't even have a bag with me!"

"I know where you hid the doll!" a voice boomed.

I turned around. Oh, no! Princess Patty!

Patty pointed a finger at Donald's big backpack. "I'll bet she hid the doll in there!"

I groaned. *Why does Patty always have to*

show up and get in the way? I wondered. She always wants to "help" us with our cases. But she tends to make things worse!

"Fine!" Jessica said. "I'll prove to you it's not in Donald's backpack!" She grabbed her brother's pack off his shoulder.

"Keep your hands off my backpack, Jess!" Donald yelled. He looked mad. He tried to back away. But Jessica had already dragged the backpack down onto the floor.

She unzipped it and started taking things out of it, one by one. "I'll show you," she told us angrily.

She pulled out a crumpled T-shirt, a camera, and a big bag of jelly beans.

"See?" Jessica said. She held up the pack. "The only other thing in here is another dirty T-shirt. Yuck!"

Jessica pushed it aside, then glared at me and Ashley. "Okay? There's nothing else in here!" she cried.

I peered into the backpack. "Hey!" I said.

"What's that shiny thing sticking out from under the T-shirt?"

"Where?" Jessica asked. She yanked the T-shirt out of the backpack.

And Princess Anna's doll rolled out of the T-shirt and onto the floor!

Jessica let out a gasp. "I don't believe it!" she shrieked. "I didn't put it there! I don't know how the doll got in there. I swear!"

Jessica's eyes welled up with tears again. "I love the doll so much," she said. "But I would never steal it. Never," she added. "I would never steal anything."

Donald looked really mad and embarrassed. He kicked at the marble floor. His boot made another big, black scuff mark on the white tile.

"Oh, all right!" he said. "I took the stupid doll. But I wasn't going to keep it. I was just going to take a picture of Jessica holding it. Then I was going to put it back. I figured she'd stop whining then."

"How do we know you were going to put the doll back?" Patty demanded.

"Patty!" I whispered. "Would you mind leaving the questioning to us?"

"Why?" she whispered back. "I'm doing a better job!"

Patty was so impossible! But I had to admit, her question was a good one.

"You just have to believe me!" Donald said. "What would I want with a doll, anyway?"

"Donald," Ashley said, frowning, "There's something I don't get. How in the world did you get the doll out of the display case?"

"Yeah," I said. "The case was locked. And the glass wasn't broken."

Donald looked confused. "Display case? I don't know what you're talking about. I didn't take the doll out of the display case. It wasn't *in* the display case!"

CASE CLOSED?

"**H**uh?" I said to Donald. "What you mean, the doll wasn't in the display case?"

"Just what I said," Donald declared. He dragged a hand through his curly red hair. "I got my seat, then came out to the lobby to get a drink and some popcorn. That's when I noticed the case was empty."

"*Empty?*" Ashley repeated. "But then where did you find the doll?"

"It was sitting right on that chair," he explained. He pointed to a chair across from the display case. The chair was right next to a door with a sign that said STORAGE ROOM.

"The doll!" a voice shrieked. "You found Princess Anna's doll!"

I turned and saw Ruska running toward us. She grabbed the doll away from me.

"Thank goodness. Where was my precious doll?" she asked.

Patty pointed at Donald. "In his backpack," she said. "*I* figured out it was in there!"

Ruska smiled at Patty. "Oh, thank you so much, young lady," she said. "Mary-Kate and Ashley must be so grateful to you for helping them with this case."

My mouth dropped open. Patty was unbelievable!

"Donald," Ashley said, "Are you telling us the truth? Did you really take the doll from the chair—and not from the display case?"

"Not from the display case?" Ruska broke in. "Of course the doll was taken from the display case. It was there until it was stolen!"

Ruska looked at Donald in a nasty way.

Boris came around the corner and heard what we were saying.

"Ruska is right," he said. "I left my post when the theater lights dimmed. I was only gone for five minutes. And the doll was in the case when I left."

"See?" Ruska insisted. "The boy must be mistaken."

"I am not! I know what I saw," Donald insisted. "When I came out of the theater, the display case was empty."

He sighed. "I figured the doll was put away while the movie was showing," he went on. "So I was about to go back in the theater. But then I saw it just lying there on that chair near that storage room door. It was easy to take it, so I did."

Ruska shook her head. "There is no need to lie, young man," she told him. "To be a thief *and* a liar at such a young age is not good."

"I'm not lying!" Donald was shouting now.

"The doll was on that chair! I picked it up, stuffed it in my backpack, and went back into the theater."

His face turned red. "I was going to grab Jessica and take her picture right after the movie. But when I came out here, all of you were waiting for us."

Ruska sighed again. "Well, all that matters is that we have the doll back. And Mr. Gudov never found out what happened. I don't think this matter needs to go any further."

Ruska cradled the doll in her arms like a real baby. She and Boris grinned at each other.

I was really happy they wouldn't lose their jobs. But I was still confused about how Donald got the doll. I was about to ask him another question—when I was interrupted.

"Donald," Patty said. "Just between you and me, how *did* you get the doll out of that locked case, anyway?"

Hey! That was *my* question!

Donald looked really angry. "For the last

time, I didn't!" he told Patty. "I don't have a key, and the glass wasn't broken. So there's no way I could have taken the dumb doll out of the case!"

Donald bent down and stuffed his things back into his backpack. Then he swung the backpack onto his shoulder. "Come on, Jessica!" he said. "Nobody believes a word I'm saying in this place. Let's get out of here before they call the police or something!"

The two of them didn't waste a second. They ran across the lobby. Then they pushed open the door and disappeared into the street.

"Let the little thieves run!" Ruska said. "I have the guest list for the premiere. It lists all the names and addresses of everyone who was invited. I will deal with the thieves and their parents later!"

She cradled the doll some more and twirled around, smiling.

"Boy, she sure does love that doll," Ashley whispered in my ear.

"Yeah," I agreed. "I'm so glad we got it back. Now Ruska and Boris won't lose their jobs."

"Mary-Kate, something's bothering me," Ashley whispered. "I just don't get it. Donald admitted he took the doll. So why is he lying about *where* he got the doll? What's the point of that?"

"I don't know," I said.

"It's a mystery," Ashley said. "And that means it will bug us until we figure it out."

Ruska straightened the doll's crown. Then she took out a key from her pocket and opened the display case.

She carefully placed Princess Anna's doll inside. Then she locked the case again.

"There," Ruska breathed. She stood back and gazed at the doll through the display case. "She is as beautiful as ever. And safe and sound again, thanks to you two detectives!"

"And me!" Patty announced.

Ruska shook hands with Ashley and me. Of

course, Patty had to come right over and shake hands, too.

"Thank you all so much," Ruska said. "I never could have found the doll on my own."

"I want to thank you, too," Boris added.

Ruska shook a finger at him. "Boris," she said, "I am very angry with you. Mr. Gudov will be here any minute. I will guard the doll until he arrives. You may go now."

Boris hung his head and left the theater.

Then Ruska turned to us. "Girls," she began, "will you guard the doll for me for just a few minutes? I need to get something out of the storage room. I'll be right back."

"Sure, Ruska," I said. "We'd love to look at her some more!"

"Right!" Ashley said. "No problem at all."

Ruska went through the door marked STOR-AGE ROOM.

"I'm going to find Brittany Barlow," Patty announced. "I want to find out where she got that boa she was wearing when she came in. I want to get one just like it."

"Good idea, Patty," I said. Now she would be out of our way for a while!

When Patty was gone, I turned to Ashley. "You know, I'm glad we cracked this case and got the doll back," I said. "But there are a lot of things that don't add up."

"I know what you mean," Ashley said. "Donald is the one who stole the doll. So how *did* those feathers and ticket stubs end up by the display case?"

"And why *would* Donald lie about where he got the doll?" I asked. "I won't be able to sleep until we figure that one out!"

Ashley gazed at Princess Anna's doll. "She really is beautiful," she said. "I can understand why Princess Anna loved her so much."

"Me, too," I said. "I'm sorry we had to miss the movie about the princess. Now we'll have to see it in a regular theater when it comes out tomorrow night. But that will be fun, too. Right, Ashley?"

But Ashley didn't answer. She was staring down at the floor. Her eyes were open wide.

"Ashley? What's wrong?" I asked.

"Mary-Kate!" she cried. "I just figured something out. Donald wasn't lying about where he got the doll!"

Huh? How did Ashley know that?

"He told the truth," Ashley declared. "There's *no way* Donald could have stolen this doll from the display case!"

8

IF THE SHOE FITS...

"**W**hat are you talking about?" I asked Ashley.

"Look!" she exclaimed. She pointed to the shiny white floor in front of the display case.

"I don't see anything," I said. I was confused. What was Ashley getting at?

"That's exactly it!" she replied. "There's *nothing* on the floor!"

I thought hard. What was the big deal about the floor? It was shiny and white and—

And then I got it. "Oh!" I cried. I stared at

the floor. "Everywhere Donald went, his boots left black scuff marks. And there are no scuff marks near the display case!"

"Right!" Ashley said. "Look at that," she added, pointing behind me. I turned and saw a winding trail of black scuff marks made by Donald's boots.

"There's a trail of marks going into the theater," I said. "And a second trail going to the concession stand. A third trail goes to the chair across the hall."

"And a fourth trail goes back out of the theater," Ashley said.

"But there's no trail going *to* the display case!" I cried. "The marble floor around it is absolutely white and clean!"

Ashley ran her fingers through her hair. "This doesn't make any sense at all," she said. "Donald didn't even go *near* the display case. He found the doll lying on a chair in the hall. But what was it doing there?"

"Yeah," I said. "Good question!"

"Someone besides Donald must have opened up the case and put the doll on the chair," Ashley said.

"But who?" I asked. "And why?"

"That's what we have to find out," Ashley replied.

We both thought hard.

"Let's ask Ruska if she has any ideas when she gets back," Ashley said. "She said she'd be back in a few minutes."

We both gazed at the doll in the display case as we thought about her disappearance.

"*She's* the only one who knows what really happened," I said. "If only that doll could talk, she could tell us what's going on around here."

I stared into the doll's beautiful blue eyes.

And then I noticed something.

I had to be wrong about what I was seeing.

Make that—what I was *not* seeing!

I stepped closer to the case so I could get a better look at the doll. I pressed my nose up against the glass.

"Oh, no!" I cried. I couldn't believe it.

"Mary-Kate, what are you doing? What is it?" Ashley asked.

I stared at her. "This isn't Princess Anna's doll! The doll in the display case is a fake!"

9

In the Dark

"**W**hat?" Ashley stared at me. "What do you mean, the doll is a fake? How do you know?"

"The *real* doll, the one that belonged to Princess Anna, has a little crack above her eyebrow," I explained.

"How do you know about that?" she asked.

"I read all about it in a magazine," I said. "There were pictures, too."

Ashley stepped up close and stared at the doll in the display case. "Mary-Kate, there's no crack above this doll's eyebrows," she declared.

"That's what I'm trying to tell you!" I said. "That's how I know it's not the real doll!"

"When we saw the doll *before* the movie started," Ashley said, "did you notice the crack was there?"

"Yes!" I exclaimed. "I definitely remember seeing the crack. I was thinking that the doll was still perfect to me, even though the crack was there."

"Good work, Mary-Kate!" Ashley said. "You have great powers of observation!"

I grinned. "Thanks," I said.

Having good powers of observation is really important for detectives. It means that you notice details—and remember them.

If I didn't notice the crack was missing on this doll, I wouldn't have known it was a fake!

"Wait a minute!" Ashley cried. "I just realized something else!"

"What?" I asked.

"This means the doll Donald took from the chair was a *fake* one!" Ashley exclaimed.

"That's right!" I said. "We took the doll from his backpack and gave it straight to Ruska. Then we watched her put it right into the display case."

"But then…where's the *real* doll?" Ashley asked, frowning.

My eyes opened wide. "It's still missing!" I cried.

"We have to find Ruska right away!" Ashley said. "We have to tell her this doll is a fake! And that the real one is still missing!"

"She's still in the storage room," I said. "Let's go!"

Ashley and I raced over to the storage room. I pulled open the door.

"Wow," Ashley said. "It's dark in there."

"Ruska!" I called. "Are you in there? It's us—Mary-Kate and Ashley."

There was no answer.

"Maybe she's in the back and can't hear us,"

Ashley said. "We'd better go hunt for her."

"We can't hunt for anything if we can't see where we're going," I said.

I stepped into the room and felt along the wall. "I can't find a light switch," I said.

Ashley ran her hand along the wall on the other side of the door. "Me either," she said.

"Maybe it's one of those old-fashioned lights with a string pull," I said. I stepped away from the wall and waved my hands in the air. I was trying to feel a hanging string.

My fingers touched a big, sticky clump of spider webs instead!

"Ugh! It's really creepy in here!" I cried.

"It sure is," Ashley said. "And I just thought of something else that's giving me the creeps."

"What?" I asked.

"We know that someone took the real doll out of the case, right?" Ashley asked.

"Right," I agreed.

"And the case wasn't broken," Ashley continued. "So the thief has to be somebody who has a key!"

"That's true," I said. "We know who has keys to the case. We asked Ruska that question right away."

"And Ruska told us that only *two* people have keys," Ashley said. "Ruska herself, and Mr. Gudov, the doll's owner."

"Well, Mr. Gudov wouldn't steal the doll," I said. "It's already his."

I gasped. "But then, that means—"

Ashley finished my sentence for me.

"It means *Ruska* has to be the one who stole the real doll!" she said.

"But that makes no sense!" I said. "Why would she hire us to find the doll if she's the one who stole it?"

"I don't know," Ashley said.

"Do you think she's the one who left the fake doll on the chair?" I asked.

"I don't know that, either," Ashley replied.

We both thought for a minute. "Well, what could her motive be for stealing the real doll?"

I asked.

"Maybe she stole it because she loves it so much," Ashley said. "She wanted to have it for her own. Or maybe she did it because it's worth so much money."

"All I know for sure is that she definitely tried to trick us," I said. "She hired us to find a fake doll! Why would she do that?"

"I think I get it," Ashley said. "Ruska must have been planning this for a while. She didn't want anyone to notice that the real doll was missing. So she had to get a fake one to put in its place. She was going to switch the dolls during the movie."

"Oh, I see!" I said. "But after she took the real doll out of the case, she accidentally left the fake doll lying on that chair in the lobby. And it got stolen!"

"So she hired us to find it," Ashley said. "When we did, she put the fake doll into the display case."

"And by the time anyone noticed it was a

fake," I said. "Ruska would be long gone—
with the real doll!"

"No wonder she wanted us to find the doll
before Mr. Gudov discovered it was missing,"
Ashley said. "He would have noticed the fake
right away!"

Click! We both heard a noise behind us. We
froze.

"What was that?" Ashley asked in a nervous
voice.

I turned around. I grabbed the storage
room doorknob and twisted it back and forth.

"Oh, no, Ashley!" I cried. "Somebody just
locked us in here!"

10

ALLEY OOPS!

"I'll bet Ruska locked us in here!" I said.

"She was probably in here with us the whole time," Ashley said.

"And when she heard us figuring out the whole mystery," I said, "she sneaked out and locked us in!"

"Maybe there's another way out!" Ashley said. "We have to look for it."

I put my arms out in front of me. I didn't want to fall on my face in the dark! I took a few scary steps.

Then I touched a wall.

"Let's follow this wall," I said.

"I'll hold onto your shoulders," Ashley said. "We shouldn't get separated."

"Good idea!"

We crept forward. After a minute, my fingers touched another wall.

"Uh-oh! I hit a dead end," I said.

"Maybe not," Ashley said. "Turn the corner and follow the new wall. Let's see where we end up."

I turned sideways and started following the new wall. Then Ashley's fingers suddenly dug into my back.

"Ow! What's wrong?" I asked.

"I heard something!" Ashley cried.

"Behind us?" I whispered.

"No! In front of us," Ashley told me. "It sounded as if someone shoved something against the wall!"

"Maybe it was Ruska shoving something against a back door!" I cried.

My hands suddenly felt something different. "There's another corner here!" I cried. "And a back hallway."

Ashley pointed over my shoulder. "Look! There's a crack of light up there. There *is* a back door!"

"I hope it isn't locked!" I said.

We ran down the little hallway toward the door. Ashley twisted the doorknob as hard as she could. It barely budged!

"Let's both push hard." I said. "I think Ruska put something heavy in front of the door so we couldn't get out."

We pushed and pushed.

The door opened! And a big trash can slid out of the way.

We stumbled outside. I caught a breath of fresh air. Boy, did it feel good to get out of that dark storage room!

"Where are we?" I asked.

"It looks like a back alley," Ashley replied.

I twisted around and saw the door we just

came through. It was marked DELIVERIES. "I think we're behind the theater," I said.

"Look!" Ashley pointed to the end of the alley. "Ruska is standing down there. It looks like she's trying to hail a taxi cab. She's holding a little suitcase."

"She must have the doll in there!" I said.

"We have to catch her!" Ashley cried.

We ran down the alley. "Try to be quiet," I said over my shoulder. "Maybe she won't hear us coming."

But it was too late. Ruska turned around and looked right at us.

"Ruska!" I screamed. "Wait!"

"You'll never get away with it!" Ashley shouted.

But Ruska wasn't ready to give up. She grabbed her suitcase. Then she disappeared around the corner of the building.

"Hurry, Mary-Kate!" Ashley screamed. "She's getting away!"

FAKE OUT!

Ashley and I pounded around the corner after Ruska. We were both gasping for breath.

We found ourselves on a busy street. Cars and buses whizzed past us.

"Stop her!" I screamed. "Somebody stop that woman!"

But there was too much other noise. Nobody heard us. The people on the crowded street moved out of Ruska's way as she ran toward them.

"She's too far ahead of us," I groaned to

Ashley. "We'll never catch her."

"If she finds a taxi, it's all over," Ashley said between breaths.

Ruska was getting farther and farther away. We were sure we were going to lose her.

"Mary-Kate, look!" Ashley cried suddenly. "There's Mr. Gudov—the doll's owner!"

I looked where Ashley was pointing. I saw the short, bald man. He was much closer to Ruska than we were.

Then I gasped—Ruska crashed right into Mr. Gudov and fell down!

Mr. Gudov leaned over. He held out his hand to help Ruska back onto her feet.

Ashley and I ran toward them so fast I thought our hearts would explode.

"Mr. Gudov!" I screamed. We were still yards away from them. "Ruska stole your doll!"

"The doll in the display case is a fake!" Ashley cried.

We dashed up to them, panting for breath.

Mr. Gudov looked confused. "What are

these girls talking about, Ruska?" he asked.

Ruska tried to smile. "Oh, they are just silly children, Mr. Gudov," she said. "Don't let them bother you."

"We're not silly children!" I cried. "We're detectives. Ruska hired us today. But she was just using us!"

"You have to listen to us, Mr. Gudov," Ashley added. "We're trying to save your doll!"

Ruska smiled again and shook her head. "Did you ever hear such a thing, Mr. Gudov? Such a crazy idea?"

Mr. Gudov still looked confused. But he seemed a little worried, too.

"Where were you going in such a hurry, Ruska?" he asked. "You were running when you crashed into me."

"Um," Ruska said. "I was…uh…."

"And what do you have in that suitcase?" Mr. Gudov went on.

"Oh," Ruska said. "I have…um…."

Mr. Gudov took the suitcase away from

Ruska. He put it down on the ground. He opened it. Then he gasped.

I leaned over and peered into the suitcase.

Yes! Princess Anna's doll was lying inside!

"Ruska!" Mr. Gudov said in a shocked voice. He picked up the doll and examined it closely. "This *is* the one and only Princess Anna doll. I know because of the tiny crack above her eyebrow."

Ashley gave me a high five.

Mr. Gudov picked up a small pile of papers from the bottom of Ruska's suitcase.

"Plane tickets!" he said. "And your passport, Ruska. You were planning to leave the country with my doll. How could you?"

Ruska made a sour face. "Oh, please!" she snapped. "The doll is worth a fortune. I planned to sell it and become a millionaire."

She put her hands on her hips and glared at Ashley and me. "The newspaper said you were great detectives. That's why I hired you to find the fake doll for me. But I never believed you were smart enough to figure out my clever plan to switch the dolls!"

"Fake doll?" Mr. Gudov said, frowning. "What are you talking about? There is only one doll like this in all the world!"

"Oh, don't look so surprised!" Ruska said. "I had a fake doll made and paid a man good money to do it! But he forgot to add the stupid crack!"

Ashley and I stared at Ruska. "My plan should have worked," Ruska complained. "I saw Boris leave his post. I knew that was my great chance to make the switch!"

"So you took the real doll out of the case," I said, "and hid it in your suitcase. But why did you leave that fake doll lying on the chair?"

"I set the fake doll down on the chair while I put the real doll in my suitcase," Ruska explained. "I was about to put the fake into the display case. But I heard footsteps. So I dashed into the storage room."

Ruska sighed. "I *had* to leave the fake doll

on the chair. I didn't have time to grab it. And then, when the coast was clear, the doll was gone!"

"So you hired us to find it," Ashley said. "That way you could put the fake doll into the display case. And you could make off with the real one."

I thought of something else.

"Ruska," I said. "Did you leave the pink feather and the orange ticket stubs near the display case? Were you trying to frame Brittany Barlow and the ticket taker?"

Ruska nodded her head. "I left those clues to frame whoever I could for stealing the doll," she said. "I thought you girls would be fooled. But *noooo*. You had to be so smart!"

Ruska let out a breath. "I heard what you said in the storage room," she said. "I locked you in! And then I tried to make sure you couldn't get out of the back door. But *noooo* again—you got out!"

Mr. Gudov sighed. "I trusted you, Ruska,"

he said. He closed the suitcase and held it with one hand. Then he wrapped his other hand around Ruska's arm. "Let's go," he said.

Mr. Gudov led Ruska back into the theater. Ashley and I followed them.

When we walked into the lobby, Patty ran up to us.

"You're lucky I was here!" she said to Mr. Gudov. "There was no guard by the doll's display case! Thanks to me, no one stole it again! I've been guarding it for you!"

Guarding a fake doll! I thought.

"Um, Patty," I said. "It's a long story. But the doll in the case isn't…"

I stopped talking when I saw Boris rush into the theater. "Mr. Gudov!" Boris ran over. "I came back to tell you the truth. I left my post and the doll was stolen! It was all my fault. I left my post and—"

Boris stopped talking. "The young detectives found the doll!" he said, staring at the display case. "How—"

Mr. Gudov opened the suitcase and took out the real doll.

Boris stopped talking again. He looked from the display case to the doll in Mr. Gudov's arms with a confused expression. "Two dolls? What? How?"

"I'll explain it all later, Boris," Mr. Gudov said. "Thank you for coming back to tell me the truth. I know I can trust you. Will you guard Ruska? I must call the police."

Mr. Gudov pointed to Ruska. "Make sure she doesn't go anyplace," he told Boris.

Boris's mouth fell open. "Of course, Mr. Gudov," he said. Boris led Ruska across the theater and sat her down on a small sofa. He kept one hand firmly around her arm.

Mr. Gudov left to find a telephone.

"What is going on?" Patty demanded.

So Ashley and I told Patty the whole story of the doll switch.

By the time we finished, Patty's mouth was wide open.

Mr. Gudov came back. "The police are on their way," he said. Then he reached into his pocket and pulled out a tiny key.

He opened up the glass case. "Now I'll return Princess Anna's real doll to her rightful place."

He took out the fake doll and studied it for a minute. "This is an excellent copy," he said. "Even I would have been fooled from a distance. But up close, you can see there is no crack above the fake doll's eyebrow."

He put the real doll into the display case.

"There you are," he said to the doll. "Back where you belong."

He turned to Ashley and me. "Thank you so much, girls," he said.

He handed us the fake doll. "I'd like you to keep this as a souvenir of your great work on this case. You deserve it for saving Princess Anna's doll for me."

"Thank you, Mr. Gudov!" I said. I glanced at Ashley. "But I think we're going to give this doll away."

"Right," Ashley said. "We know a little girl who loves Princess Anna's doll even more than we do!"

"It's true that Donald stole the doll—even if it was a fake," I said. "But I really believe his story. He was only going to take a picture of Jessica with the doll and then return it."

"Yeah," Ashley said. "I believe him, too. We should let them know what happened."

"We can get her address from the invitation list," I said. "Let's find them tomorrow."

"And I know what we should do after that," I said.

"What?" Ashley asked.

"Since we missed the premiere of 'The Disappearing Princess'—" I began.

"We'll go see it tomorrow!" Ashley finished. We gave each other high fives.

And the Trenchcoat Twins cracked another case—Hollywood style!

Hi from the both of us,

Where could someone hide an elephant? That's what Ashley and I had to find out! Someone stole Maysie—the baby elephant—from the circus. And Maysie was the star of the show!

Ashley and I had to find her fast—before opening night. So we got our dog, Clue, on the case. Clue has the best nose in the business. She could sniff out an elephant in no time!

But Clue had a really bad cold! Her super-duper sniffer wasn't working too well. And opening night was just hours away!

Want to find out more? Take a look at the next page for a sneak peek at The *New* Adventures of Mary-Kate & Ashley: The Case Of The Great Elephant Escape.

See you next time!

Love,

Ashley Olsen + Mary-Kate Olsen

A sneak peek at our next mystery…

The Case Of The
Great Elephant Escape

"WOOF! WOOF! WOOF!" Clue began to jerk on the leash. She pulled so hard the leash flew out of Ashley's hands!

"Clue!" we both yelled. "Come back!"

But Clue was running as fast as she could.

"She must smell Maysie!" I said. "Go, Clue! Lead us to her!"

We ran through the circus city. Suddenly Clue skidded to a stop. She stood in front of a huge trailer. It must have been three times as big as the others.

In fact, *this* trailer was big enough to hold an elephant!

I looked at my sister. I could practically feel my eyes popping.

"Ashley," I said, "I think we just found Baby Maysie!"

Ashley pointed to a fancy sign on the door of the huge trailer. It read, "Home of the World's Biggest Man—Clyde Big."

"And look at this note," Ashley said. She pointed to a piece of paper that was taped on the door. It read, "PLEASE do not disturb—I'm resting."

"There can't be an elephant *and* Clyde in there, too," I said, frowning. "It's a big trailer, but it's not *that* big. So why would Clue take us *here*?"

Ashley sighed. "I think I know why." She scratched Clue behind her ear. "Clue's cold must be messing up her sense of smell," Ashley explained. "First she took us to Marlon the clown, and now Clyde Big. She just can't sniff out Maysie. It's our super-duper snooper's first blooper!"

I petted Clue. "Poor dog," I said. "You probably have the same cold that Clyde Big has."

"WOOF! WOOF!"

"Clue's barking again," Ashley said.

"No kidding." I bit my lip. "I know you think her nose isn't working," I said, "but I say we should give her another chance. Let's go!"

Clue bounded off again. Ashley and I ran after her.

We followed Clue to a smaller tent behind the big top. We poked our heads through the narrow opening flap.

I didn't see any elephants. Instead, the tent was full of fuzzy little dogs in frilly tutus!

Clue trotted over to us. Ashley grabbed her collar. "I take it back," she whispered. "Clue doesn't have a cold. She has the flu! She mixed up an elephant's scent with dogs. Yikes!"

Yikes was right! I was starting to get really worried. We didn't have any leads. And Clue's super nose wasn't helping us out at all, either.

How were we ever going to find Baby Maysie—and solve this mystery?

Mary-Kate & Ashley
Ready for Fun and Adventure? Read All Our Books!

THE NEW ADVENTURES OF MARY-KATE & ASHLEY ™

❑ BBO-0-590-29542-X	The Case of the Ballet Bandit	$3.99
❑ BBO-0-590-29307-9	The Case of 202 Clues	$3.99
❑ BBO-0-590-29305-5	The Case of the Blue-Ribbon Horse	$3.99
❑ BBO-0-590-29397-4	The Case of the Haunted Camp	$3.99
❑ BBO-0-590-29401-6	The Case of the Wild Wolf River	$3.99
❑ BBO-0-590-29402-4	The Case of the Rock & Roll Mystery	$3.99
❑ BBO-0-590-29404-0	The Case of the Missing Mummy	$3.99
❑ BBO-0-590-29403-2	The Case of the Surprise Call	$3.99
☑ BBO-0-439-06043-5	The Case of the Disappearing Princess	$3.99

THE ADVENTURES OF MARY-KATE & ASHLEY ™

❑ BBO-0-590-86369-X	The Case of the Sea World™ Adventure	$3.99
❑ BBO-0-590-86370-3	The Case of the Mystery Cruise	$3.99
❑ BBO-0-590-86231-6	The Case of the Funhouse Mystery	$3.99
❑ BBO-0-590-88008-X	The Case of the U.S. Space Camp™ Mission	$3.99
❑ BBO-0-590-88009-8	The Case of the Christmas Caper	$3.99
❑ BBO-0-590-88010-1	The Case of the Shark Encounter	$3.99
❑ BBO-0-590-88013-6	The Case of the Hotel Who-Done-It	$3.99
❑ BBO-0-590-88014-4	The Case of the Volcano Mystery	$3.99
❑ BBO-0-590-88015-2	The Case of the U.S. Navy Adventure	$3.99
❑ BBO-0-590-88016-0	The Case of Thorn Mansion	$3.99

YOU'RE INVITED TO MARY-KATE & ASHLEY'S ™

❑ BBO-0-590-76958-8	You're Invited to Mary-Kate & Ashley's Christmas Party	$12.95
❑ BBO-0-590-88012-8	You're Invited to Mary-Kate & Ashley's Hawaiian Beach Party	$12.95
❑ BBO-0-590-88007-1	You're Invited to Mary-Kate & Ashley's Sleepover Party	$12.95
❑ BBO-0-590-22593-6	You're Invited to Mary-Kate & Ashley's Birthday Party	$12.95
❑ BBO-0-590-29399-0	You're Invited to Mary-Kate & Ashley's Ballet Party	$12.95

- -

Available wherever you buy books, or use this order form
SCHOLASTIC INC., P.O. Box 7502, 2931 East McCarty Street, Jefferson City, MO 65102

Please send me the books I have checked above. I am enclosing $_____ (please add $2.00 to cover shipping and handling). Send check or money order—no cash or C.O.D.s please.

Name _____

Address_____

City_____State/Zip_____

Please allow four to six weeks for delivery. Offer good in the U.S.A. only. Sorry, mail orders are not available to residents of Canada. Prices subject to change.

High Above Hollywood the Olsens Are Playing Matchmakers!

Check Them Out in Their Coolest New Movie

Mary-Kate
Olsen

Ashley
Olsen

Billboard DAD

One's a surfer. The other's a high diver.
When these two team up to find a new love
for their single Dad by taking out a person-
als ad on a billboard in the heart of
Hollywood, it's a fun-loving, eye-catching
California adventure gone wild!

Now on Video!

DUALSTAR
VIDEO

Don't Miss
Mary-Kate & Ashley
in their 2 newest videos!

You're Invited to MARY-KATE & ASHLEY's

Costume Party

You're Invited to MARY-KATE & ASHLEY's

Mall Party

Available Now Only on Video.

Two Times the Fun!
Two Times the Excitement!
Two Times the Adventure!

Check Out All Six *You're Invited* Video Titles...

...And All Four Feature-Length Movies!

And Look for Mary-Kate & Ashley's
Adventure Video Series.

DUALSTAR
VIDEO

Listen To Us!

Ballet Party™

Birthday Party™

Sleepover Party™

Mary-Kate & Ashley's Cassettes and CDs
Available Now Wherever Music is Sold

It doesn't matter if you live around the corner...
or around the world...
If you are a fan of Mary-Kate and Ashley Olsen,
you should be a member of

MARY-KATE + ASHLEY'S FUN CLUB™

Here's what you get:
Our Funzine™
An autographed color photo
Two black & white individual photos
A full size color poster
An official **Fun Club™** membership card
A **Fun Club™** school folder
Two special **Fun Club™** surprises
A holiday card
Fun Club™ collectibles catalog
Plus a **Fun Club™** box to keep everything in

To join Mary-Kate + Ashley's Fun Club™, fill out the form
below and send it along with

U.S. Residents – $17.00
Canadian Residents – $22 U.S. Funds
International Residents – $27 U.S. Funds

MARY-KATE + ASHLEY'S FUN CLUB™
859 HOLLYWOOD WAY, SUITE 275
BURBANK, CA 91505

NAME:_____

ADDRESS:_____

CITY:_____STATE:_____ZIP:_____

PHONE: (___) _____BIRTHDATE:_____